The Fou

Enid Blyton

*Illustrated by Joyce Smith
and David Dowland*

SPARROW
BOOKS

A Sparrow Book
Published by Arrow Books Limited
17-21 Conway Street, London W1P 6JD

An imprint of the Hutchinson Publishing Group

London Melbourne Sydney Auckland
Johannesburg and agencies
throughout the world

First published by Lutterworth Press 1962
Sparrow edition 1981
Reprinted 1984

Printed and bound in Great Britain by
Anchor Brendon Ltd, Tiptree, Essex

ISBN 0 09 926640 7

CONTENTS

GRANNY COMES TO TEA

"**G**RANNY'S come to tea!" called Mummy as soon as John and Sarah came running in from school. "She's in the garden—go and see her."

"Oh good!" said John. "I'll show her the lovely new scooter Daddy's given me!"

"And I'll show her my new baby doll," said Sarah. "The one that can speak! Oh— and where's our new barrow? Granny will like to see that."

Granny was sitting out in the garden, enjoying the sunshine. She smiled when Sarah and John came up, Sarah with her new doll, and John dragging the barrow behind him as he rode on his new scooter.

"Well, well—new toys again!" said Granny. "What a BEAUTIFUL doll, Sarah! Who gave you that—Auntie Sue?"

She smiled when Sarah and John came up

"Yes," said Sarah. "She's always giving us lovely presents—and it isn't even my birthday!"

"You know," said Granny, "*I* could tell you about some children who have only a dirty little dish-cloth wrapped round a stick for a doll."

"Why haven't they a proper doll?" asked Sarah in surprise. "I've six dolls, not counting my dolls' house dolls."

"Billy and Betty haven't a Daddy, and their Mummy has very little money," said Granny. "They are often hungry, and hardly ever go out for a walk, or to play, as you do."

"But why doesn't their Mummy take them out for walks, as ours does?" said John.

"Because she has to go out to work all day, and she leaves them behind in the one room she has," said Granny. "And from breakfast-time to tea-time they have nothing to eat, because there is no one to see to them. Sometimes a neighbour looks in, but that's all."

Sarah's eyes filled with tears. "Granny, can't you help them?" she said.

"I do," said Granny. "Whenever I hear of any sick, lonely, unhappy children, I do all I can to help them to be well and happy. And, you see, when I come to visit you, and see your beautiful toys, and the lovely food Mummy gets for you, and the warm fires, and kisses and hugs, I can't help remembering these other children. I suppose *you* wouldn't like to help me, would you?"

"Oh *yes*, Granny!" said Sarah. "We'll come with you and play with the poor little things."

"No—they need much more than a play-mate," said Granny. "They need a lovely long holiday by the sea—and that costs money. Do you think you could set to work to do little jobs, and earn some money to help me to send little Betty and Billy away to the sea?"

"But what little jobs could we *do*?" said Sarah. "I don't know any that would earn me money."

"And we're always so busy," said John. "I don't know how we'd find the time."

"Ah well—I rather thought you would say that," said Granny, getting up. "I'll ask your two cousins to help me—Sam and Susie—they're a kind-hearted pair, bless them."

"Granny, we *will* help you," said Sarah.

"But do tell us how to get some jobs! I don't want Sam and Susie to help you, and not us. Please sit down, Granny."

"Well, Sam and Susie are a grand pair of children," said Granny, sitting down again. "They already do such a lot of things for other people, that I hardly like to ask them to help in this too. But I know they would say yes, at once!"

"*We're* saying yes, too," said Sarah. "Granny, can we do jobs for any of your friends? Then if we get paid we will give you the money for Billy and Betty. Truly we will."

"Very well," said Granny, smiling. "But mind now—once you take on something, you must go on with it! I'll tell you the kind of jobs that Sam and Susie do, when they want to earn money for anything."

"What do they do?" asked John.

"Well, Susie does the washing-up after tea," said Granny. "Her Mummy pays her five pence a time—that's thirty-five pence a week. She runs errands any day—and gets ten pence an errand. She even goes shopping for some of the neighbours on Saturday morning, and they pay her thirty pence for fetching a full basket of goods, and fifteen pence for a small basket of goods."

"I wouldn't mind doing that," said Sarah. "It would be fun—if people would *let* me do it!"

"As for Sam, he does quite a lot of jobs," said Granny. "He cleans his father's bicycle once a week—that's a fifty-pence job if it's done properly. And he takes three dogs for a walk each evening—three puppies—at ten pence a walk."

"What does all that money go to?" asked John. "Do they buy toys for themselves?"

"No. They are saving up to help sick or hurt animals," said Granny. "You know how fond of birds and animals they are. They have a money-box, and I can tell you that it is getting very full! I could hardly pick it up last time I saw it!"

"Granny, we *will* help," said Sarah. "Truly we will. You just see! We'll be every bit as good as Sam and Susie at earning money. It sounds quite easy, really."

"Well—talk it over with Mummy and see what she says," said Granny, getting up. "I'll hear what you've done when I come to tea again next week—so you'd better begin straight away!"

And off went Granny to say good-bye to Mummy. The two children looked at one another. "We'll begin as soon as we can," said Sarah. "Now—let's make a few plans, John. How can *we* earn some money?"

"WHATEVER were you two talking about with Granny?" said Mummy, when they came in from the garden. "You all looked so serious!"

"Granny wants us to help her with a poor little boy and girl she knows," said Sarah. "They simply must go away for a holiday by the sea, Mummy."

"Well, darling, I'd be very glad if you *would* do something like that," said Mummy. "But you always seem so busy—why, you hardly have time to run an errand for *me* sometimes! And as for you, John, you always say you haven't time even to clean your new scooter! So how will you find time to help Granny? And HOW are you going to help her?"

"Well," said John, "There's Daddy's bike,

for instance. Would Daddy let me earn thirty pence a week if I kept it clean?"

"He certainly would!" said Mummy. "And if Sarah would run errands for me when I'm busy, I would pay her fifteen pence each errand."

"Oh, Mummy—we'd soon earn money then!" said Sarah. "Then Billy and Betty could go away for a lovely long seaside holiday. Mummy, isn't it dreadful, they are left alone all day while their Mummy goes out to work!"

"They aren't the only children who need help," said Mummy. "There are plenty of unhappy children in the world—and I think it's right that *happy* children should try to help them. Look—here's Daddy—tell him about Granny's idea."

So the two children told him, and he nodded his head, pleased. "Just like Granny," he said. "Always helping other people. Well, well—to think she has managed to get you two to help her! I was beginning to think you were really a very selfish little pair."

"We're *not*," said Sarah, and she went very red in the face. "You wait and see! We're going to do a lot of jobs of all kinds—and we'll put the money into our money-box, and you'll see—we'll soon send that little girl and boy away for a holiday."

"Right," said Daddy. "Thirty pence a week to you if you keep my bicycle clean, John. And thirty pence a week to you, Sarah, if you keep the bicycle shed swept out—it gets so dirty."

"But where shall I get a broom?" said Sarah.

"That's up to you," said Daddy. "I've no doubt Mummy has a stiff broom. And, John, if you want to earn any *more* money, you can do a spot of weeding for me. That bed by the front gate is full of weeds—I'm really ashamed of it."

"How much for that?" asked John.

"Well—if it's really *properly* done, I'll give

you fifty pence," said Daddy. "But mind—I'm not paying for bad work—only for good work!"

Daddy went off, whistling, looking rather pleased. Well, well—to think that John and Sarah wanted to do something for other people! *That* was a change—they were usually so selfish.

"Too many aunts and uncles giving them presents and spoiling them," thought Daddy. "Now I wonder—WILL John clean my bicycle each week—or will he do it just once and then not bother any more?"

Sarah went to her mother. "Mummy—would you trust me to do the washing-up sometimes?" she said. "I promise to be very, very careful. Granny says that Susie does it for her mother, and gets paid five pence a time. *She's* helping Granny too—to send that boy and girl away on holiday, you know."

"Yes—I will trust you to do the washing-up if you'll promise me to do it very, very

"I promise to be very, very careful"

carefully," said Mummy. "You know how you hurry over jobs—well, you *can't* hurry over washing-up, you'll break things if you do."

"Oh, I'll do it very, VERY carefully," said Sarah. "I can do it just as well as Susie, I'm sure!"

"Well, listen—you shall have five pence a time, just like Susie—but if you break any-thing you must give me back the money you have earned," said Mummy. "Then I can buy a new cup, or saucer, or whatever it is you break. That's fair enough, isn't it?"

"Well, as I shan't break ANYTHING, it's quite fair!" said Sarah. "Any other job, Mummy? I do want to earn a lot of money—just like Susie!"

"Right," said Mummy. "Well, if you want to earn any *more* money, you can help me to darn Daddy's socks. You have learnt how to darn at school, and that would be a great help to me. I'll pay you fifteen pence a sock, because Daddy's socks do get rather big holes in them."

"But I don't like darning," said Sarah.

"All right—it's up to you!" said Mummy. "If you want to earn as much as you can, you will have to take what jobs are offered to you!"

Sarah went off, pleased. Why, she could earn a great deal of money every week. She counted it up for herself. "Washing-up—thirty-five; darning two socks — thirty;

sweeping out Daddy's shed—thirty; running errands, say fifty pence. How much is all that?"

She wrote it all down, and then added up the money. "Good gracious! I should earn at *least* one pound forty-five! I'm sure that's more than Susie would earn! Won't Granny be pleased!"

She went to get her book to read. It was an exciting story, and she settled down comfortably on the garden seat. She had read just two pages when Mummy called her.

"Sarah! Will you run down to Mrs. Day's, please, and tell her I'd be glad if she could come in and help me tomorrow morning?"

"Oh, Mummy—MUST I?" said Sarah. "I'm reading. Can't John go?"

Oh, Sarah, Sarah! Is *that* the way to earn money? Have you forgotten your plans already?

3.   *SARAH ISN'T VERY KIND*

SARAH settled down to her book again. Mummy didn't call any more. But soon Sarah heard voices, and sat up to listen. Were visitors here?

"Oh, it's only Sam and Susie," she thought. "I hope they don't see me here. I do want to finish my book."

But they did see her, and after they had gone to say how-do-you-do to their aunt, Sarah's mother, they came to find Sarah.

"Hallo, bookworm," said Sam.

"Hallo," said Sarah, hardly looking up.

"Don't bother to talk to us," said Susie, with a laugh. "We're just off to do an errand for your mother."

Sarah looked up at once. "What errand?" she said.

"Just popping down to Mrs. Day's cottage to ask her to come up tomorrow to help your mother," said Sam. "We said we'd go for nothing, but your mother's giving us fifteen pence each, because she knows we're collecting for something."

"Fifteen pence *each*—thirty pence!" said Sarah.

"Threepence *each*—sixpence!" said Sarah.

"Well, there's *two* of us going," said Sam. "Good-bye, bookworm!"

And off they went, laughing. Sarah was very angry. They had taken *her* errand—and would have money *she* could have earned. She went crossly indoors to her mother.

"Why did you ask Sam and Susie to go down to Mrs. Day's?" she said. "You knew I was planning to earn money for Granny. Now *they'll* have it!"

"Well, you didn't want to go," said Mummy. "And I couldn't find John to ask. I was very glad when Sam and Susie came along. They brought me some eggs their chickens had laid—six beauties, look. I paid them five pence for each egg, so they made thirty pence straightaway!"

Sarah went very red. Thirty pence for eggs from their chickens—and now thirty pence for an errand! It was too bad.

"Can *I* have some chickens to keep?" she said. "Of my very own, like Sam and Susie? Then *I* could sell eggs."

"Oh, darling—you would never look after them properly," said Mummy. "Don't you remember your poor little canary? You forgot to clean out its cage, you forgot to feed it or give it water—and I had to give it away. You would never remember to feed hens or look after them."

"It was John's fault too," said Sarah, sulkily. "It was his canary as much as mine."

"That makes it worse," said Mummy. "Two forgetful children instead of one! Look —here are Sam and Susie back again already, on their bicycles. Get your box of chocolates and ask them to have some."

But Sarah went off in a huff. Offer her precious chocolates to Sam and Susie when they had earned money *she* could have earned? No! She would go and hide till they had gone!

So off she went—and when at last she came out of hiding, she went to find John. But he was nowhere to be seen.

"Mummy—where's John?" she asked.

"Down by the front gate, I should think," said Mummy. "He said he'd like to get on with weeding the bed there, and earn fifty pence."

Away went Sarah to find him. But he wasn't by the front gate. She looked at the very weedy bed. John had pulled up a few weeds, certainly—they lay in an untidy heap. But that was all he had done. Where was he?

She shouted for him. "JOHN! JOHN—where are you?"

A head popped over the left-hand wall. "Here I am! Playing with Tony! What do you want?"

"Oh, nothing. Mummy said you'd gone to weed this bed—but it doesn't look as if you've done much! I expect by the time you get down to it again, a whole lot of new weeds will have grown up!"

"Well, Tony has a new Red Indian suit," said John. "He called me in to see it. It's smashing! Anyway, what have *you* been doing all this time? Running errands? Washing-up? I bet you haven't!"

"Don't you talk to me like that, lazy-

A head popped over the left-hand wall

bones!" said Sarah. "Pretending to weed and only pulling up half a dozen! I could have done the whole bed! I've a good mind to!"

"Don't you dare to touch it!" shouted John, angrily. "That's *my* job. You go and do yours. Go on—go and darn or something. *You're* the lazy-bones, not me. *I* saw you lazing on the garden-seat, reading your book!"

"I'll smack you when you come back over the wall!" cried Sarah, and ran up the path to the house, wishing she *could* smack her brother! All right—she would show him she could earn money first! What could she do?

"I'll sweep out that shed!" she thought. "That will show John I can do something before he does!"

So off she went to find a broom. There was one in the garage, so she took that. She opened the shed-door—Daddy's bicycle was inside, looking very dirty—and as for the shed, it was full of dust, and bits and pieces, and old papers! What a mess!

"I'll sweep everything on to the bicycle!" thought Sarah. "Then John can clear the mess up before he cleans it. That will serve him right!"

So she swept the shed as clean as possible, except for the corner where the bicycle stood. Oh dear—what a mess she left that corner in! All her sweepings went over the bicycle— what a very unkind thing to do!

IT WAS supper-time when Sarah had finished her sweeping. She shut the door of the bicycle shed, put away the broom, and went to wash her hands. She would tell Daddy she had already swept out the shed once—he would be pleased!

John came running in just in time for supper. He hardly had time to wash before Daddy was sitting at the head of the table.

He too, had come in just in time!

"Well!" he said, beaming round at everyone, "I've been gardening at the very bottom of the garden, and I've built a magnificent bonfire. I shall light it tomorrow, and burn all the rubbish."

"Oh—so *that*'s where you've been," said Mummy. "I looked out of the window, and I couldn't see you or John—only Sarah on the garden-seat."

"I was next-door, having a fine time," said John.

"Dear me—I quite thought you said you were going to start on that weedy bed by the gate," said Daddy.

"Oh yes—I did start on it," said John. "I expect I'll be able to finish it tomorrow."

"No, you won't, my boy," said Daddy. "That bed will take a long time to do, if you pull up *all* the weeds. I'll have a look after supper to see how much you've weeded."

"Oh don't bother, Daddy," said John, at once. "I'd rather you waited to look at it till it's all nice and tidy."

"Ha! You've only done a little tiddly bit," said Sarah, unkindly. "I went to see!"

"Tell-tale!" said John, and aimed a kick at Sarah under the table. Unluckily the kick hit Daddy on the ankle, and he glared at John.

"Leave the table! You can go without your

"What do you mean by kicking me like that?"

supper. What do you mean by kicking me
like that?"

"I meant it for Sarah," said John, scared.

"Well, you must be the only boy in this
town who would be mean enough to kick his
own sister," said Daddy. "Go up to bed!"

"Sarah, you shouldn't tell tales!" said
Mummy. "I'm ashamed of you."

"I'm ashamed of them both," said Daddy,
unhappily. "I don't believe either of them will

put themselves out to earn a single penny for Granny. What's the matter with them? Sam and Susie aren't like that!"

"They're spoilt," said Mummy, sadly. "But I did think they were turning over a new leaf when they were so keen to do all kinds of jobs to help that poor little girl and boy."

Sarah began to cry. "I DO want to help," she said. "I swept out the bicycle shed tonight. I know I didn't go that errand for you, Mummy, and I'm sorry. But I did sweep out the bicycle shed."

"Well, I'm very pleased to hear *that*," said Daddy, looking more cheerful. "I'll go straight out after supper and see how beautifully you've done it."

Oh dear—Sarah remembered how she had swept all the dirt and rubbish over Daddy's bicycle so that John would have a harder job to clean it! Now what would happen? Daddy would certainly be very angry!

"Oh don't go now, dear—go and see it

tomorrow morning—it's getting dark," said
Mummy, and Sarah heaved a sigh of relief.
She would get up early and sweep out the
shed properly, putting all the rubbish out of
the door, and into a barrow, instead of over
Daddy's bicycle.

"All right," said Daddy. "I'm glad to
hear that *one* of our children has done a job of
work. I'll go up and talk to John—then he
can come down and have his supper, if he's
going to behave himself."

John came down, looking very sorry for
himself. "Sorry I tried to kick you, Sarah," he
said, rather sulkily. "Mummy, I've told Daddy
I'll clean his bicycle first thing tomorrow—
and I will too, you'll see! I'll set my alarm
clock for half-past seven!"

Sarah sighed. Half-past seven! Oh dear—
she would have to be even earlier than that if
she meant to sweep the rubbish right out of
the shed!

But Sarah had no alarm clock. How could

she wake herself? She couldn't ask Mummy to wake her, because at once Mummy would ask her why.

"Perhaps if I go to bed immediately after supper, I'll wake up very early." she thought. So, much to her mother's surprise, she announced that she was going to bed at once.

"But, darling—don't you feel well?" said her mother, anxiously.

"Quite well, Mummy—but I'd rather like to be up early tomorrow," said Sarah.

"I'll wake you," said John, at once.

"No. I'll be up earlier than half-past seven," said Sarah, and that made everyone look MOST surprised.

"Ha—doing some job or other to earn money, I suppose," said Daddy, looking pleased.

Sarah went up to bed at once, and undressed. Bother, bother, bother! She would have to be up so early! Why had she been so silly as to play that nasty trick on John? She cuddled down in bed and tried to go to sleep at once. But she couldn't, of course!

She woke up to hear John's alarm clock ringing loudly in the morning. Oh dear— now John would be down in the shed first. Still, maybe she could dress more quickly than he could. So out she jumped and was soon dressed. She passed John's bedroom door as she crept over the landing—and dear me, through the crack she saw that he was still fast asleep! Good—now she could do what she wanted to, and have plenty of time to do it!

5. *SARAH DOES SOME JOBS*

SARAH was soon sweeping out the rubbish in the shed. She had to put Daddy's bicycle outside first, and then it was easy to sweep everything out of the door. She grinned to herself as she thought of John still asleep in bed.

"I shan't wake him!" she thought. "It will serve him right if he's late and doesn't clean Daddy's bicycle after all!"

She put all the rubbish into a barrow, and wheeled it to the bonfire. It was still smoking. Sarah threw everything on to it. There! Now she had earned thirty pence!

Daddy came down the garden to the shed.

He saw Sarah by the bonfire, and called to her.

"Have you seen John? I thought he said

he was going to clean my bicycle early this morning. I want to ride it instead of taking the car."

"He was asleep when I passed his door," said Sarah. "*I* got up as soon as I heard his alarm going off."

"Why didn't you wake him, then?" said Daddy, looking suddenly cross. "You *know* he said he wanted to be up early. I expect he was so fast asleep that he didn't wake. Don't you think it was rather mean of you not to wake him? And what is all this rubbish you're burning?"

"It's from the bicycle shed," said Sarah. "I've just swept it all out and I thought it could burn on your bonfire, Daddy."

"I thought you said you'd swept out the shed *yesterday*," said Daddy, puzzled.

Sarah didn't know what to say. She *had* swept the shed the evening before—but she certainly hadn't swept the rubbish *out*—she had swept it all over Daddy's bicycle! But she couldn't possibly tell him that! So she stood there silent, looking very guilty.

"Well—here's the thirty pence I promised," said Daddy. "But I might have given you fifty if you'd been nice enough to wake up John, and let him get on with *his* job! It's a good thing it's Saturday and you don't have to go to school!"

John came running down the garden just then, horrified to think that he had overslept. "Why didn't you wake me, you mean thing!" he said to Sarah. "Daddy, I'm sorry I haven't done your bike yet. I'm going to do it this very minute!"

"I should think so!" said Daddy. "I had a good mind to tell your cousin Sam to come along and clean it for me, when I heard you were sound asleep in bed. But you can't do it now. It's time for breakfast. Do it immediately afterwards."

Sarah slipped away. She felt ashamed of herself. It *was* mean not to have wakened

John. Well, anyway she had earned thirty pence—that was something.

"I'll pop it into our money-box straightaway," she thought. "And after breakfast I'll ask Mummy if she wants any errands run."

So after breakfast was over and she had, as usual, made her own bed, she ran to her mother.

"Any errands, Mummy?" she said.

"Well, how nice to hear you ask that!" said her mother. "Yes, darling. I want you to go to the grocer's and collect these things on my list. And I'll leave you the breakfast things to wash up, if you like—that will be another job."

Sarah set off to the village with the list. She really felt rather important, for Mummy usually did the shopping. She went the rounds of the shops, remembered everything, and went home with her basket full. Mummy was very pleased.

Sarah set off to the village

"That's fifteen pence for you," she said. "And you have remembered everything! Very good. Now, if you want to earn another fifteen pence, Mrs. Hall over the road wants an errand done."

Sarah was beginning to feel very pleased with herself. She had earned thirty pence for sweeping out the shed, and fifteen pence for doing Mummy's shopping—and perhaps Mrs.

Hall would give her another fifteen—that would be sixty pence already! Granny would be delighted.

Mrs. Hall was very kind. She gave Sarah her shopping list, which wasn't a very long one, and a basket to bring everything back. "And the bar of chocolate I've put down on the list is for *you*," she said. "Just a little reward!"

Sarah loved chocolate—but oh dear, if she took the chocolate as payment for doing the shopping, she wouldn't have earned any money for the little boy and girl!

But Mrs. Hall wouldn't know that! She could eat the chocolate, and tell her mother that Mrs. Hall hadn't given her any money for doing her errand! She set off down the path—and then into her mind came the picture of a pale little girl and boy sitting all alone for hours, in a dreary room, waiting for their mother to come and give them something to eat!

She rushed back to Mrs. Hall. "Mrs. Hall —would you mind if I *didn't* buy the chocolate bar? You see, I'm trying to earn money to send an ill little girl and boy away for a seaside holiday. May I have the money instead?"

"Bless your kind little heart!" said Mrs. Hall, and gave her a hug. "Of course you may. The chocolate bar I put down for you costs thirty pence, so keep that money for the little boy and girl."

"But I only expect *fifteen* pence for an errand," said Sarah, honestly.

"Well, you shall have the extra fifteen pence for your kind heart!" said Mrs. Hall. "And I'll tell all the neighbours what you are doing—they'll give you errands too, and my word, you'll soon have your money-box full— and that little girl and boy will go joyfully off to the seaside!"

Sarah felt so happy that she danced all down the road. She was glad she hadn't been greedy and taken the chocolate to eat. Now she would have thirty pence for their money-box, instead of fifteen. It was fun doing jobs for people—it wasn't a nuisance. It was fun, it really *was*!

6. *JOHN IS* VERY *BUSY*

JOHN wasn't finding it much fun doing jobs for his father. He was late in going down to the bicycle shed after breakfast, and oh dear—when he arrived there, the bicycle was gone! He went back to his mother and asked her where it was.

"Well, Daddy *told* you he was going to ride it this morning," said his mother. "You couldn't expect him to wait till ten o'clock. I'm disappointed in you, John."

John didn't like his mother to look at him sadly, shaking her head. "Shall I go and weed that bed?" he said. "Or is there anything I can do for you first, Mummy?"

"You go and weed the bed, and show Daddy you're not as lazy as he thinks you are," said Mummy. "And if you want to do a job for me quickly now, you can go and pick some peas for me—and pod them, too."

"I don't mind picking them, but I do hate podding them," said John.

"I see—you just want to do the jobs you like, and leave me the ones you don't like?" said Mummy. "Very well. Perhaps Sarah will pod them for me. I am so busy this morning, and I expect she will like to earn a little more money. She really is doing very well this morning."

"No, Mummy—it's all right, I'll pod them," said John, in a hurry. He picked up a basket and ran down the garden to the row of peas. The sun was very hot, and the pea-pods were rather difficult to pick—if John wasn't careful he pulled the whole plant away from the pea-sticks! He was very hot and thirsty when he had finished picking and podding.

He took the peas back to the house. "I'm so thirsty I could drink a whole bottle of

lemonade!" he said. "May I get one,
Mummy? And how much money may I
have for picking the peas—and for podding
them too?"

"Well, you may have fifteen pence for picking so many pea-pods, and twenty pence for
shelling them," said his mother. "You may
also have a bottle of lemonade—but if you
like to drink water instead, I will give you the
cost of the lemonade—twenty-five pence—
and you can add that to your earnings."

"Oh, but I DO want some lemonade," said
John, dolefully.

"Well, have it," said Mummy. "I just
thought that you might like the idea of
having an extra twenty-five pence for your
money-box. The sooner you get it filled, the
sooner that little girl and boy you told me
about will be able to have their seaside
holiday—poor little things!"

John went to fetch the bottle of lemonade.
He was just going to take off the top, when a

picture came into his mind. He saw that little girl and boy all alone in their room—*they* had no lemonade—or lovely garden—or even anyone to play with. Without a word, he put back the lemonade, and went to his mother.

"I've changed my mind, Mummy," he said. "I'd rather have the twenty-five pence for our money-box after all."

"That's my own kind boy," said Mummy, and her eyes shone. She gave John a kiss, and then counted out fifteen pence, twenty pence and twenty-five pence.

"That adds up to sixty pence!" said John. "Mummy, I'm getting on, you know. Our money-box will soon go clinkity-clink—such a nice sound!"

He put his money into the money-box that he and Sarah were sharing. "It feels a *bit* heavy," he told his mother. "But it will soon be VERY heavy—you wait and see!"

"I will, dear," said his mother.

"I'll just go and get a drink of water," said John. "I really *do* feel so thirsty! Then I'm ready for another job, if you like."

"No, not just yet. Go and have a little read," said his mother. "You can take two biscuits to eat from the tin. Hallo, here comes Sarah —she must have finished Mrs. Hall's shopping. Hallo, dear—how did you get on?"

"Oh, Mummy, it was *fun*!" said Sarah. "Mrs. Hall gave me fifteen pence for the shopping I did—and oh, Mummy, she gave me *another* fifteen pence too—but not for shopping. You'll never guess what it was for!"

"Chocolate for you?" asked Mummy, who knew that Mrs. Hall was very kind.

"Well—in a way," said Sarah. "But when I said no, I'd rather not have the chocolate, she gave me the extra money and she said it was for my kind heart! Wasn't it nice of her?"

"Very nice," said Mummy. "And I'm glad you didn't have the chocolate. John didn't have the lemonade I offered him, either—so he had twenty-five pence for *his* kind heart!"

"Well, really it's for Billy and Betty," said John. "I just felt I didn't want the lemonade —because *they* couldn't have any, however much they longed for it."

"That's the way dear old Granny thinks about things," said Mummy. "How pleased she will be when I tell her all this."

John ran off to weed the bed by the front gate. It was very hot there, for the sun shone down fiercely. He panted and puffed, but he wouldn't give up. Soon the bed was half done, and very nice it looked too.

"How the flowers show up, now the weeds are gone," thought John proudly. "Why, this bed is beautiful now! I wouldn't mind weeding another one for Daddy. My word, I'm not doing badly today. I'm earning quite a lot of money. I wonder if I've earned more than Sarah."

Somebody came by and stopped to watch

the busy little boy. "Hey, John!" said a
voice. "That's a fine job of work you're doing!
I wish you'd come and do a bit of weeding
for *me*. I'd pay you well."

"Oh, Mr. Brown—you made me jump!"
said John. "I'd love to do some weeding for
you. I'm collecting money for something,
you know. I'll come this very afternoon!"

Soon the bed was half done

JOHN
IS VERY SILLY

AFTER dinner was over that day, John yawned. "I feel tired!" he said. "I think I'll go and snooze in a deck-chair, Mummy."

"I thought you were going to weed at Mr. Brown's," said his mother. "Have a little rest, then you must go. You promised, you know."

John stretched himself out in the sun in a low deck-chair. Oooooh—that felt nice! His back ached from bending over the bed by the front gate, and it was nice to lie in peace.

He was soon fast asleep, of course! Mr. Brown waited and waited, but John didn't come. He went to the front gate to look for him—and who should come by but Sam, John's cousin.

"Hallo, Sam!" said Mr. Brown. "Are you off to a job?"

"No, I've just finished one," said Sam. "Did you want one done, sir?"

"Well, yes, I did," said Mr. Brown. "Your cousin John said he'd do a bit of weeding for me. My back's bad, you know, and I can't bend down."

"I'll go and fetch him for you, sir," said Sam. "And if you like I'll do some weeding too—I can see that your garden needs it!"

"Right—there's plenty of work for you both," said Mr. Brown, pleased. "I'll show you what to do when you come back."

Sam went off to his cousin's house. He found John fast asleep in the deck-chair. He nudged him. "Hey, wake up, John! WAKE UP! Have you forgotten you've some work to do?"

John half-opened his eyes. "Stop jabbing me," he said, crossly. "I'm tired. I've been working all the morning."

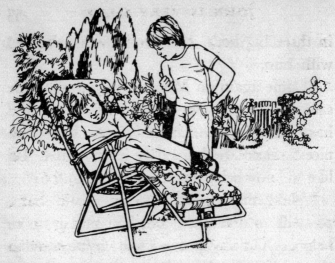

"Hey, wake up, John! WAKE UP!"

"But Mr. Brown said you were going to do some weeding for him," said Sam. "I've come to fetch you."

"Well, tell him I'll be along tomorrow," grumbled John and shut his eyes again. Sam went away. "Lazy thing!" he thought. "Still, it's grand for *me*—I shall earn quite a lot of money weeding this afternoon!"

So he did! He was a fine worker, and a quick one, and he cleared away all the weeds in three big beds. Mr. Brown was delighted with him.

"Come again on Monday, if you will," he said. "After tea—or better still come and have tea with me first. My cook bakes the nicest chocolate buns I've ever tasted. I'd like to know what *you* think of them, too!"

"Well, thanks, Mr. Brown," said Sam, pleased. "I'd like the job. I'm saving up to help my Granny to send two children off to the seaside, you know."

"Let me see—you did three big beds—and left not a single weed. I think you deserve thirty pence for each bed," said Mr. Brown, taking out his purse.

"Oh, thank you very much!" said Sam. "I'll be along on Monday, sir, and try those chocolate buns!"

Just as Sam was going out of the gate, he saw John in the distance. Should he tell John what he had earned? No, better not—he would be so cross! John didn't see him, and went straight to Mr. Brown's. It was four o'clock—goodness, what a long time he had been dozing! Why hadn't he leapt up from his chair when Sam jabbed him with his finger!

Mr. Brown was tying up a loose bush by the gate. He was surprised to see John. "Well, young man, *you're* a bit late in the day!" he said. "Your cousin has been here all afternoon and weeded three big beds for me!"

"The mean thing!" said John, angrily. "*I* was going to do those. You know I was."

"Well, if you'd come along as you said you would, there would have been quite enough work for you both," said Mr. Brown. "And don't stand glaring at me like that, young man. It's your own fault. You promised to come—and you broke your promise—so Sam got the whole job, and deserved it too."

"How much did he earn?" asked John, red in the face.

"Ninety pence," said Mr. Brown. "And

he is coming again on Monday. He's a good lad, that."

John went home, angry with himself. He wondered what Sarah was doing. She had been very, very busy! Mrs. Tomkins had called in to see her mother, and when she heard that Sarah was busy earning money to help her Granny, she was very interested. "Would she like to earn some money this afternoon?" she asked. "If so, I wonder if she would take my twins for a walk in the park? I'd pay her fifty pence."

"She would love to, I'm sure," said Sarah's mother, and called the little girl in from the garden. Sarah beamed. She liked the twins very much, and she was glad to hear of such a pleasant way of earning more money! Really, this was a very good day!

She fetched the twins and away they went to the park. They fed the ducks, and played cricket with a bat and ball the twins had brought, and had a really lovely time. When

Sarah took the twins home, they kissed and hugged her.

"Take us again," they said. "Mummy, can Sarah take us again?"

"Yes, if she will," said Mrs. Tomkins, paying Sarah fifty pence. "And I'll pay you each time, Sarah dear, for I hear that you are saving up to help two poor little children."

"Yes—Billy and Betty," said Sarah. "Thank you, Mrs. Tomkins. I did enjoy earning that money!"

She ran home, very pleased. She went to find John, to tell him her news. He looked sulky, and didn't even smile. "You get all the luck!" he said. "That horrid Sam went to Mr. Brown's and did *my* job—and was paid for it—ninety pence! And then *you* go and have a lovely afternoon in the park, and get paid for it! It's just too bad! I've a good mind to stop trying to earn money."

SARAH was very pleased to feel their money-box getting heavier and heavier. She wondered what job she could do next. Ah—what about washing up the tea-things!

"If I do the washing-up for you after tea, Mummy, shall I earn some money?" she said. "I promise to be very, very careful."

"Oh, darling—I think you must be tired now—you've been running errands, and taking care of children all day it seems!" said her mother. "You might break something. Do the washing-up for me tomorrow."

"No. I *do* want to do it today!" said Sarah. "If I break anything I'll pay you for it out of my earnings. But I shan't break a thing, *You'll* see!"

So after tea Sarah carried the tea-things carefully into the kitchen and ran the hot water into the bowl. She put in some soap powder and swished the water about to dissolve them. There—nice foamy water to wash up everything!

John came out to see what she was doing. *Another* job! *More* money for Sarah! He felt cross as he saw his sister carefully rinsing out each cup and saucer.

"I'll help too," he said, and took up a saucer.

"No—don't!" said Sarah at once. "This is *my* job, and I won't have you telling Mummy you did half of it. You've been lazy all day, so you can go *on* being lazy!"

John held on to the saucer as Sarah pulled at it. It was so slippery with water that it slid out of their fingers and fell to the ground— crash! It shattered into many pieces.

"Now look what you've done!" shouted Sarah. "Broken a saucer! Well, *you'll* have to pay for it out of *your* earnings, because this was *my* job!"

It slid out of their fingers and fell to the ground—crash!

She was crying when Mummy came out to see what had broken. "It wasn't my fault," sobbed Sarah. "John grabbed at the saucer, Mummy. Oh, Mummy, shall I have to give you some of my earnings back?"

"No, Sarah," said Mummy. "We won't count this job—you've only just begun it, so I'll finish it. I think I've an extra saucer we can use, so this broken one won't matter.

John, go away, I'm not very pleased with you today."

John marched off, blinking away tears. How MEAN when he had been trying to do a job! Well, no, he hadn't *really* been trying—he had just been cross because Sarah was doing so much more than he was. Poor Sarah! Now she would lose the money for washing up.

He went back. "Sarah," he said, "I didn't mean to break the saucer. I'm sorry. *I'll* pay for it!"

"You need neither of you pay," said Mummy. "I know you've both been working hard! Accidents *will* happen! Now go and get out the snap cards, and shout 'Snap' at each other for a while. That's the best game of all for people who feel snappy!"

Well, that made them both laugh, of course, and away they went to get the cards— and Mummy finished the washing-up, with a funny little smile all over her face!

Daddy came in while the two children were playing cards. "Hallo, hallo!" he said. "And how are the two wage-earners getting on today?"

"Not badly," said Mummy, who had come in to watch the game. "They've weeded—and washed up—and taken children to the park—and run errands. . . ."

"Jolly good," said Daddy, pleased. "By the way, John, I've heard of rather a nice job for you if you'd like to do it—or you and Sarah could do it together."

"What job?" asked John, at once.

"Well, you know old Mrs. Houston? She has a lovely spaniel—a black one—and a poodle too. The old lady has gone rather lame lately, and can't take the dogs for their evening walk. She wondered if you would like to take them. She would pay you thirty pence a time."

"I'm a bit afraid of dogs," said Sarah.

"Well, *I'm* not. I simply LOVE them!" said

John, in delight. "Oh I DO wish we had a dog
of our own. Daddy, when can we have one?
Sarah wouldn't be afraid of them if we had
one of our own."

"I don't *want* to take Mrs. Houston's dogs
out," said Sarah. "I'd be afraid they might
bite me, Daddy. I do *like* dogs—but I just
wish they hadn't such a lot of teeth."

Mummy laughed. "Well, when you or I
smile at a dog, I expect it thinks *we* have
rather a lot of teeth!" she said. "Daddy, I
think that's a lovely idea. Sarah, why don't
you go with John, and take a dog each?
You could have the little poodle—it's so tiny
that it's like a toy. You really *couldn't* be
afraid of that!"

"No, don't you bother to come, Sarah,"
said John. "I can manage both—and then
I'd not have to share the thirty pence, would
I, Daddy?"

"Well—I *will* come then," said Sarah, who
badly wanted to earn some more money. "Bu

only if you'll promise not to let the dogs bark at me, John."

"I can't promise that," said John. "Don't be silly. That dear old spaniel wouldn't hurt anyone, and I've never once heard him bark. And you could carry that poodle in your pocket, it's so small—well, *almost* carry it there—fancy being afraid of nice dogs like those!"

"Well, I'll try the job and see what it's like," said Sarah. "But I really AM afraid of dogs, even nice ones."

"Then it's brave of you to take on half the job," said Daddy, and gave her a hug. "I like brave children—especially when they belong to *me*! Come along now—I'll play snap with you too—Mummy, you play as well. We'll pretend we are dogs snap-snap-snapping at each other all the time but no biting, mind!"

G RANNY came to tea the next day,
which was Sunday. She smiled at
John and Sarah and gave them a
loving hug each. "Well," she said, "and how
have my two wage-earners been getting on?
Does your money-box clink yet?"

"Oh *yes*, Granny—listen!" said John, and
he shook the box hard. "And feel it—isn't it
getting heavy? Doesn't it make a lovely
clinkity-clink too?"

"Well, well—what in the world have you
been doing to make it heavy so quickly?"
said Granny, and she listened, smiling, as the
two children told her about all the jobs they
had done.

"Splendid!" she said. "Dear me, you
are just as good and clever as Sam and
Susie!"

"Are we *really*?" asked Sarah, very pleased.

She had always been afraid that Granny liked Sam and Susie best.

"Yes. There isn't a pin to choose between my four nice grandchildren," said Granny. "All kind, all working to help other people, and all happy in doing it. I've felt Sam and Susie's money-box and theirs is heavy too— but no heavier than yours. Susie has a job she likes very much."

"What is it?" asked Sarah.

"She feeds the neighbour's cat each day!" said Granny. "The people have gone away, and as the cat hates leaving its home, they don't like to ask anyone to take it while they're away—so they've left it behind, because Susie offered to look after it and feed it. And you know, she doesn't much like cats!"

"How funny!" said John. "*We* are going to take dogs for walks—and Sarah doesn't like dogs!"

"Well, I daresay that dogs will like *Sarah*!" said Granny, giving Sarah a loving pat.

"She's just the kind of child they like—gentle and kind, and with a nice soft voice."

Sarah was so pleased when she heard Granny say that. She knew she *wasn't* always gentle and kind—but how good it was to hear Granny say that she was! Granny always said truly what she thought—even when it was something *not* very nice to hear!

"Do dogs *like* gentle voices?" she asked.

"Oh yes," said Granny. "Too sharp or loud a voice frightens dogs, or makes them angry—but a kind, soft voice makes them run to you and whine in pleasure. You try it!"

"Well, I will," said Sarah, making up her mind to speak very gently to the poodle and the spaniel when she and John took them out. Perhaps they would make friends with her then, and not bark at her or bite her. John was all right with dogs—they always loved him—he wasn't a bit afraid of them!

They went to see Granny off at the front gate. She kissed them good-bye and patted their shoulders. "Thank you for your help, my dears," she said. "I never, never thought you would work so hard to help me in my job of looking after unhappy people. I'm proud of you!"

The next day was Monday, so there was no time to do any jobs—except the one in the evening! John was so much looking forward to taking out the dogs that he dreamed over his lessons, and, dear me, when his teacher rapped on his desk and said, "Wake up, John, and tell me the answer to this sum! Quickly now!" what *do* you suppose John said?

He blinked at his teacher, and said, "Er— the answer is *two dogs*, Miss Hester!"

Everyone roared with laughter, even Miss Hester. After that, John woke up a little and tried to put dogs out of his mind. "I do love them so," he thought. "If only, only, ONLY I had one of my own!"

That evening he and Sarah set out for the

house next door. Mrs. Houston was sitting
in her front garden with her two dogs beside
her. The poodle yapped at once, and Sarah
drew back in fear. The spaniel didn't move,

Mrs. Houston was sitting in her front garden

but lay and wagged her stumpy tail, looking
up at her out of kind brown eyes.

"Hallo, dears," said Mrs. Houston. "I'm
afraid I can't get up to welcome you, because
I'm rather lame today. It's so kind of you to

take my dogs for their evening walk. They do so miss it. This is Lassie the spaniel—and this is Topsy the poodle. Say how do you do, Lassie and Topsy."

And to the children's delight, each dog held out a front paw most politely for the children to shake. Sarah was so surprised and delighted that she quite forgot to be afraid! They all shook hands or paws, and then the dogs ran to the gate, and stood there as if to say, "Do come along!"

"They won't need leads, if you'll take them down the lane and into the woods," said Mrs. Houston. "They are very obedient dogs, and will come at once if they are called."

"They won't go into the road and be run over, will they?" said Sarah anxiously.

"Oh no—they are trained to keep on the pavement, and only to cross when you do," said Mrs. Houston. "Now—off you go, all of you!"

Down the road went the two children with

the dogs. Lassie the spaniel kept close to John's ankles. He liked to feel the soft nose bumping his legs every now and again. Topsy the poodle danced in front and looked round at them as if to say, "Isn't this fun! Oh, I DO love a walk!"

"Isn't she a darling?" said Sarah, in delight, quite forgetting that she didn't like dogs. "She's like a toy dog come alive. Topsy, Topsy, come here!"

And up to her danced the happy little dog, her eyes shining, her tail wagging. She licked Sarah's hand and gave a little loving yap.

"She looks as if she's smiling when she opens her mouth like that," said Sarah. "I like her, John. I do really."

"You'll like dear old Lassie too, before long!" said John. "You just wait and see!"

10

A HAPPY TIME

"WELL?" said Mummy, when the children came back, after their walk, each with fifteen pence in hand. "How did you get on? I'm sure the dogs didn't growl or snap or bite, did they?"

"Mummy, they were *lovely*," said John, his eyes shining. "Lovely! Dear darling Lassie kept with me all the way, and Topsy danced the whole time, just in front of Sarah. She simply *loved* Sarah."

Sarah looked very happy. "I tried out my voice on Topsy and Lassie," she said. "Just to see if Granny was right, and if they liked a soft sort of voice. And, Mummy, Topsy came and snuggled up to me, whining in delight— and Lassie kept on and on licking my hand."

"Well, you can't be afraid of dogs after that," said Mummy.

"I still am—of *other* dogs," said Sarah. "I love Topsy, but I almost think I love Lassie more—you've no idea what kind loving eyes she has, Mummy. Almost as kind as yours!"

Soon the dogs grew to know the children so well that they often came into their garden to find them. Topsy danced all round and about, and ran off with this and that—but Lassie went round solemnly to everyone, and gave them a loving lick—and then, as often as not, lay down by John, and laid her soft, shining black head on his feet.

"If ONLY I could have a dog!" he said to himself in bed each night. "One like Lassie, black and silky and with brown eyes that almost talk—and a stump of a tail that wags happily. Oh, if ONLY I could have a dog of my very very own!"

It was a very happy time taking out the two dogs for Mrs. Houston, but a happier time was still to come, for, when she went away for three days she asked the children's mother if the children could have the dogs to stay.

"I'll pay them the same as I pay the man who usually looks after them," she said. "Two pounds fifty a day, which includes their food. They can put the money into their money-boxes, to help to pay for the holiday for Billy and Betty they keep telling me about."

"Do you think you *can* look after Topsy and Lassie properly?" asked their father, looking at the two delighted children. "It means such things as cleaning out the kennels, giving them their meals, providing them with clean drinking-water—and brushing their coats. And, of course, taking them for walks."

"Daddy!" said John, his eyes shining like stars. "Of *course* we can! Sarah isn't frightened of dogs any more—are you, Sarah? So she can help me. Oh, DADDY! To think I'll have Lassie all to myself for a bit!"

Daddy was very pleased with the two children—they looked after the two dogs very well indeed. They kept the kennels clean, full of good straw—they washed the water bowls each day and put in fresh water—they brushed the dogs and combed them till they looked good enough to win the first prize in any dog-show!

The dogs were very happy. The poodle adored Sarah, and even wanted to sit on her knee as soon as she sat down. The spaniel loved them both—in fact she loved the whole family, and went round at breakfast-time licking every one of them in turn.

"That's her morning kiss," said Daddy, patting her as she licked him. "She's seen *you* give us a morning kiss, and she thinks she'd like to do the same."

"Darling Lassie!" said John, and stroked her soft silky head. "Fancy being *paid* to look after you! I'd do it just for love, you're so sweet."

The children were sad when Mrs. Houston came back and the dogs went to live at her house again. But it really seemed as if the

"Rolling on the lawn with both the dogs"

dogs thought that they lived at the children's house, for they were always in and out!

"Who would have thought that Sarah didn't like dogs, and was afraid of them?" said

Granny, the next time she came to see them all. "Look at her rolling on the lawn with both the dogs! Well, well—they did Mrs. Houston a good turn in looking after the dogs —and Lassie and Topsy have certainly taught Sarah that dogs are creatures to be loved, and need not be feared."

"Our money-box is getting *really* full now, Granny," said Sarah, coming up. "Feel it. It's so heavy that it weighs down our hands!"

"You're good, kind children," said Granny, taking the box. "I didn't really think you would work so hard for me, when I told you about Billy and Betty. Shall I open your box and see how much you have? I think maybe we shall soon have enough between us to arrange for those little children to have their holiday."

"Oh *yes*—let's open the box!" cried John. "We've put in such a lot lately—because of looking after the dogs."

"And I've been doing a lot of darning for Mummy," said Sarah. "Look at my pricked fingers! I'm clumsy at darning, aren't I, Mummy?"

"No—you're very good at it," said Mummy. "But you're not very kind to your fingers! You should see the socks she has darned, Granny—really, you couldn't tell which of us darned those socks—Sarah is as good as I am!"

Sarah was very pleased. It was worth a good many pricked fingers to hear Mummy praise her like that! "Granny—let's open the box," she said.

So Granny passed the heavy box to Mummy, and she fetched the key and slid it into the little lock. She opened the box and gasped in surprise.

"Look—it's almost full to the top with pennies and fifty-pence pieces and pound notes! I'll count them up and see what they come to."

Well, will you believe it—the money came to twenty-six pounds and seventy pence! No wonder everyone shouted for joy. What a truly marvellous thing!

11

PLENTY OF MONEY
FOR BILLY AND BETTY!

THE two children stared in astonishment at the money that Mummy had emptied out on to the table. More than twenty-five pounds—all made from the little jobs they had done! They couldn't believe it.

"Granny—is it enough to send those little children away to the sea for a holiday?" asked Sarah, anxiously.

"I've my papers about it here in my bag," said Granny, taking out some letters. "It will cost ten pounds to send them away for two weeks. Susie and Sam have opened their box, and . . ."

"Did they earn a LOT more than we did?" asked Sarah, hoping that she and John had earned as much as their cousins.

"They made eighteen pounds and ten pence exactly," said Granny. "So you earned more.

Sam and Susie started off very well indeed—but their money goes on other things as well—like helping hurt animals."

"It was taking care of the two dogs next door that *really* made the box quite full," said John. "We were so well paid for that."

"Oh, Mummy has told me of the many, many things you both did," said Granny. "I'm proud of all my four grandchildren—it's not many grandmothers that have such kind ones, you know! Well, well, well—I AM pleased! I didn't for one moment think that you four would get so much money for me."

"But you haven't quite enough," said John, worried. "You need over three pounds more to have thirty pounds."

"And that's just what Daddy and I are going to put in!" said Mummy, opening her bag. "Granny, you'll let *me* share in this, won't you? And Daddy, too? Please don't leave us out. There—I'll give you three pounds—and thirty pence. Does that make thirty pounds?"

Solemnly John counted all the money again. When he had finished he smiled in delight. "Yes! That's exactly thirty pounds, Granny. When will Billy and Betty go away?"

"Soon now," said Granny. "Will you come and see them off at the station with me? Their mother is going with them, of course, but she is able to pay for herself. I expect she will like to say thank you to you for all your kindness."

"I don't really want any thanks," said John. "I've enjoyed doing the jobs so much, Granny. I was a bit silly at first, you know— but I did like doing the jobs."

"So did I," said Sarah, her eyes shining. "Especially taking out the two dogs—and looking after them for three days! Oh, Granny—I feel as if I don't want to stop earning money for you, now I've begun. Isn't there anything else we can earn money for —and give it to you to use?"

"That's the loveliest thing you've ever said to me, Sarah," said Granny, and dear me, how surprising, Sarah saw that Granny had tears of joy in her eyes! "I'll think about it, darling. I certainly would be very, very glad of your help—and Sam's and Susie's too. There are the little blind children who need help—there are sick or hurt animals—there are all kinds of people who are lonely and sad . . ."

"Dear Granny, we will *all* help you," said Mummy, suddenly. "You're so kind—we can't help wanting to help you in all the things you do! Oh, what a good thing you asked Sarah and John to do those jobs for you. I don't think they'll ever stop now!"

"We never will stop," said Sarah, hugging Granny. "And we'd love to come and see Billy and Betty off on their holiday. When will it be?"

"Oh, they can go in a few days now that I have the money," said Granny, happily.

"Perhaps even tomorrow, if their mother can get them ready. I'll let you know, dears."

Then Granny said good-bye, gave them each a hug and a kiss and went trotting down to the front gate, looking very happy indeed. "What a dear little person she is!" thought Mummy. "And *what* a good idea it was of hers to get Sarah and John and Sam and Susie to help. I didn't know the children had so much kindness in them—I'm really proud of them all!"

That evening the telephone rang, and Mummy went to answer it. It was Granny, sounding very excited.

"What do you think! I've been able to arrange for Billy and Betty to go TOMORROW! They are so excited that I am sure they won't sleep tonight! Their mother is getting their clothes ready, and has been given time off to go with them. They are all so very happy and excited—it's the first holiday they have ever had in their lives!"

"Here's the train—good-bye, good-bye!

"What time is the train?" asked Mummy, very pleased. "We'll be there to see them off."

"It goes at half-past ten," said Granny. "What a good thing it's Saturday tomorrow, so that the children can all come! I'll see you then."

And what a joyful time that was on the railway station the next day! Granny came along in a taxi with a young, tired-looking

Wave, children, wave—good-bye!"

woman—the children's mother—and two thin, pale children, so excited that they couldn't keep still for a moment.

Sam, Susie, Sarah and John were there, with their mothers—and each child had bought a bar of chocolate or a bag of sweets to give to the children to eat on their journey. Sarah was shocked to see how pale and thin they were—and so little for their age.

"You are kind, ma'am," said the tired mother to Sarah's mother. "I can't thank you enough—and your dear children too for all they did to earn money for our holiday. God bless you, I say, God bless you. Here's the train—good-bye, good-bye! Wave, children, wave—good-bye!"

And off puffed the train with the little family. The four cousins waved till it was out of sight. "I DO hope they have plenty of sunny days, and a LOVELY time," said Sarah. "It was worth doing all our jobs to see those two excited little children—it really was!"

12.   *A WONDERFUL SURPRISE!*

GRANNY took the four children into the dairy to have an ice-cream each. She beamed at them all. "Well now —what is it to be—vanilla, chocolate or strawberry?"

They each chose their favourite, and began to talk of the jobs they had done. "You earned more money than we did," said Sam. "Much more."

"Ah yes," said Granny, "but you have to remember that you and Susie help other things as well. Half your spare money goes to sick or hurt animals."

"I liked doing those jobs," said Sarah. "I did really. So did John."

"The one I liked the best was taking out the two dogs next door," said John, spooning up his chocolate ice-cream. "Granny, you'd have loved those dogs—a silky spaniel with

87

brown eyes—and a dancy, adorable little poodle."

"I know them well," said Granny. "And by the way, John, you'd better go and see Mrs. Houston soon. You may find that she has a few more dogs!"

"Goodness—is she going to keep Kennels for dogs?" said John. "You know—take dogs in and board them and look after them? I'd like that. I might go and help."

"We'll go and see Mrs. Houston as soon as we can," said Sarah. "I like dogs now, though I never did before. I can't *think* why I was ever afraid of them!"

"Thank you, Granny, for those *delicious* ice-creams," said Susie. "We'll have to get back now. We're going out with Mummy."

So the little party broke up, and they all went home, feeling happy whenever they thought of the two excited little children in the train. Perhaps they could send two *more* children away for a holiday sometime, thought Susie. She would have to ask Granny about that. It was really quite easy to do jobs and earn money! Anyone could do that. What a pity that more children didn't know what fun it was!

Sarah and John walked home together. John suddenly give a deep sigh and Sarah looked at him in surprise.

"What a sigh! Is anything wrong?"

"No—not really," said John. "It's only that I didn't know how lovely it was to have a dog—those two we looked after were such dears. I do miss them. If ONLY Daddy would let me have a dog of my very own, I would be PERFECTLY happy!"

"That reminds me—we'd better pop in to see Mrs. Houston's new dogs," said Sarah. "The ones Granny told us about. I expect she's going to take care of some for her friends."

They walked in at Mrs. Houston's gate, and at once heard the yapping of the little poodle in the distance. "That's Topsy," said Sarah. "Lassie—where are *you*?"

Mrs. Houston limped out of a nearby shed, and called to the children. "Hallo, dears! I'm glad you've come."

"Granny said you had some new dogs," said John. "May we see them?"

"Yes—come into the shed," said Mrs. Houston, and they went in with her. A large box lay in a corner under a window. In the box, on an old blanket, lay Lassie the spaniel. She looked up at them with loving eyes and gave a proud little whine. Four tiny black heads beside her moved as she whined.

"Oh—PUPPIES!" cried John. "Oh, Lassie has puppies—four of them. Are *these* your new dogs? Oh, Mrs. Houston, aren't they *lovely*? Oh, may I pick one up?"

"Not yet," said Mrs. Houston. "They're too little. I am going to sell three of them as soon as they are old enough. I know of very good homes for them."

"Oh, Lassie has puppies—four of them"

"What are you going to do with the fourth?" asked John. "Keep it for yourself?"

"No," said Mrs. Houston. "I'm going to give it away. I thought *you* might like one of these puppies for your own, John."

John could hardly believe what Mrs. Houston had said! He stared at her, and his heart began to beat very loudly. Could it be

true? A puppy for *him*—for his very own?
Oh, what a wonderful, wonderful surprise!

"But Daddy wouldn't let him have one,"
said Sarah, sadly. "He'll say no, Mrs.
Houston."

"Well," said Mrs. Houston. "I've already
asked him if John can choose one of these,
and he said 'Yes, certainly—John deserves a
dog now—he has earned one!' Your Daddy
told me that himself."

John was so happy that he couldn't say a
word. He just looked down at the puppies,
little black squirming things with silky coats
—and one was going to be HIS! It couldn't
be true! He turned to look at Sarah, and she
flung her arms round him.

"It's what you ALWAYS wanted, John—and
I'm so glad for you. You'll let me share a tiny
bit of him, won't you? I love dogs now too,
you know."

"He shall be *our* dog," said John. "Which
one shall we have? Oh, they're all so sweet!"

"Choose one in a week's time when you can see them better," said Mrs. Houston. "I've heard all about the many many jobs you've done, as well as looking after my dogs —and I think you both deserve to have one of Lassie's puppies. The new little pup will have a good master and mistress—he'll love you both!"

"And we'll love *him*!" said John.

Yes, you will, John and Sarah. Wait till you have him, and he lives with you, goes walks with you, trusts you, is sad when you are sad, and happy when you are happy— what a friend you will have then!

But you deserve him, you really do! You didn't want any reward for your hard work —but you won't say no to the thing you wanted most—a Dog of Your Very Own!